# Rosy's Balloon

igloobooks

One day, in summer, Rosy
got a shiny star balloon.

"It's very special," said her mother.
"It's a present from the moon."

Rosy's lovely, bright balloon
floated in the air.

# This igloo book belongs to:

......................................

igloobooks

Published in 2015
by Igloo Books Ltd
Cottage Farm
Sywell
NN6 0BJ
www.igloobooks.com

HUN001 0215
2 4 6 8 10 9 7 5 3 1
ISBN 978-1-78440-291-4

Illustrated by Steve Whitlow
Written by Alex Michaels

Printed and manufactured in China

She held it by a ribbon
and took it everywhere.

All too soon, the sunshine went
and the wind began to blow.

It tugged at Rosy's star balloon.
"Hold on tight, Rosy. Don't let go!"

The rough wind blew and storm clouds grew
and Rosy could not hold on.

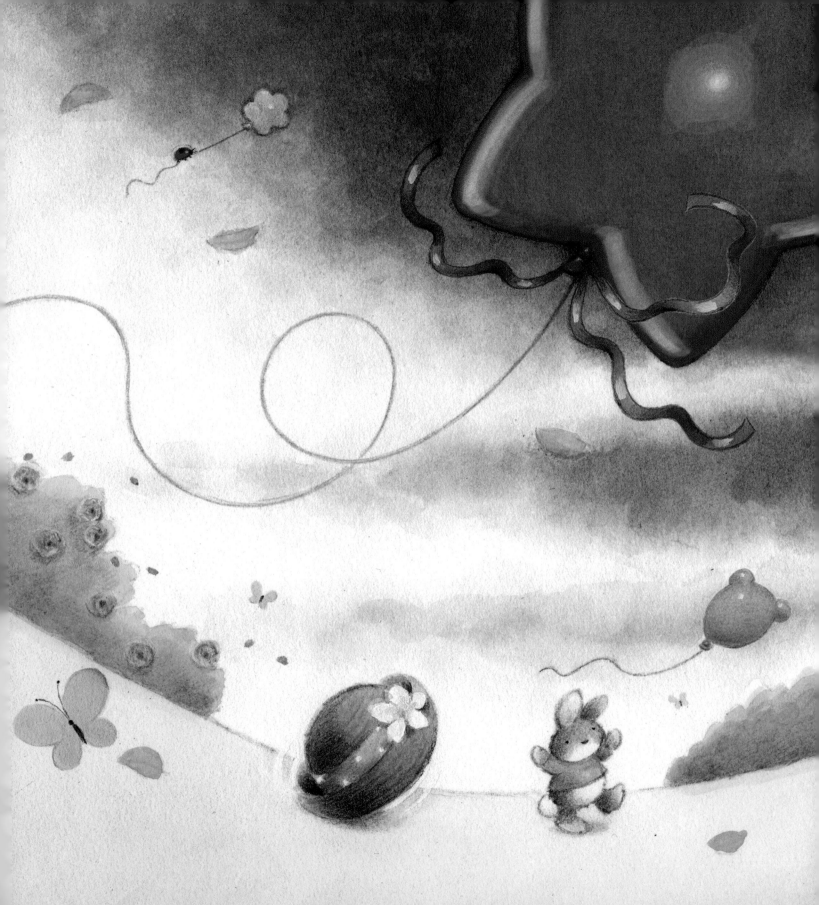

Whoosh! went the wind, it tugged and pulled.
Suddenly, the star balloon was gone.

Up, up, went the balloon,
to the tallest treetop.

Its pink ribbon tangled and
the star balloon stopped.

"Caw!" went the crow, with his feathers so sleek.
Suddenly, he took the ribbon in his beak.

Off he flew into the stormy sky
and carried the star balloon up high.

Suddenly, lightning crashed
and thunder clapped.
The crow's feathers ruffled
and his blue wings flapped.

"Caw, caw!" cried the crow
and he let the star balloon go.

"My star balloon is gone," sobbed Rosy.
"I'll never see it again."

"There, there," said her mother, holding Rosy tight,
as the soft sunlight gave way to the night.

Rosy's mother said that the moon was alone
and he cried for the star balloon to come home.

"Look up," she said. "Look up high.
There's your star balloon, twinkling in the sky."

"Goodnight," said Rosy. "I'll see you soon."
She blew a kiss to her special star balloon.

"Goodnight, Rosy.
Sleep tight."